The Lonely Chick

Archie retreated to the rock feature and crept into his warm little hidey-hole amongst the rocks. The lonely little chick watched the goslings with their parents, the black swan cygnets with theirs and the ducklings…

"Where do I fit in?" Archie wondered miserably.

Look out for more books by Sylvia Green!

Sylvia Green

The
Lonely Chick

Illustrated by Sophie Keen

SCHOLASTIC

For Anne

Scholastic Children's Books,
Euston House, 24 Eversholt Street,
London NW1 1DB, UK
a division of Scholastic Ltd
London ~ New York ~ Toronto ~ Sydney ~ Auckland
Mexico City ~ New Delhi ~ Hong Kong

First published in the UK by Scholastic Ltd, 2006

10 digit ISBN 0 439 95050 3
13 digit ISBN 978 0 439 95050 3

Printed and bound by Nørhaven Paperback A/S, Denmark

1 2 3 4 5 6 7 8 9 10

Papers used by Scholastic Children's Books are made
from wood grown in sustainable forests.

Chapter 1

Archie
"Why am I different?"

Archie scrambled to his feet, ruffling his soft, fluffy, yellow down. He blinked in the sunlight streaming through the open door of the duck-house.

Mum was looking proudly at her ten newly-hatched, fluffy, yellow youngsters cheeping and bustling around in the nest. But when her eyes rested on Archie she paused. "Oh my," she said. "That's a bit unusual."

Archie was too excited to notice her expression. He looked over from the open door to his brothers and sisters. "Hey, you guys, what say we explore a bit?"

Hatching had been a pretty exhausting business, all that pushing and stretching to break out of the eggshell, and Mum had kept them in yesterday. Archie had felt safe and warm snuggled under Mum's soft feathers with his brothers and sisters. But now he was ready to face the world.

He led the way to the door and stared out at the vast expanse of grass and trees.

"Hey, look at all this," he cheeped.

His brothers and sisters crowded round him.

"Wow, it's big," said Aaron.

"Huge," said Amanda.

Mum quacked softly behind them. "It's called Deanswood Landscape Gardens. And it's your home, ducklings."

Archie ran down the ramp and his brothers and sisters scuttled out behind him. He couldn't wait to check out this exciting new world.

"What's that, over there, Mum?" Archie asked.

"It's another duck, dear," said Mum patiently. "Only it's a Mallard, not an Aylesbury duck like us."

"Is that what we are then? Aylesbury ducks?"

Mum ruffled her lovely white feathers. "Yes, dear, we're Aylesbury ducks."

"And what's that?" asked Archie eagerly, looking around him. "And those two, over there? And that, Mum. What's that?"

Mum patiently named the trees and the flowers. Then she named the pair of geese grazing on the grass and a human called Jim, who was riding a noisy machine that was cutting the grass.

"Now come on, ducklings," she said. "Form a line and follow me."

Archie eagerly joined in, in the middle of the line, and they all marched in single file after their mother. They followed her down a short, grassy slope and stopped in front of a HUGE shimmering thing. "Here we are," she said. "This is the lake."

They all ran forward to look. "Wow! Cool," cheeped Amy.

"Neat," said Alec.

Archie wasn't so sure. It looked dark – and wet.

"OK, ducklings, time for your first swim," said Mum. "In you go."

Archie watched in horror as Anna and Adam jumped straight into the water.

"What are you doing?" He rushed in front of the others. "Don't jump in there. Don't do it, guys!"

"That's silly," said Mum. "We're ducks. We like nothing better than a good swim. Now come on, all of you. In you go."

Another white duck swam over to them and Mum introduced them to their father. "In you come, ducklings," he encouraged them.

Father-duck watched proudly as, one by one, the rest of the ducklings jumped in. Then there was only Archie left on the bank.

Mum gently nudged Archie with her bill. "In you go, dear."

"Come on. Jump in!" called Andy.

"It's lovely," cheeped Abbie.

Archie looked at them happily swimming round and round in the water. They all seemed to be enjoying it. And Father-duck was looking at him expectantly now.

Perhaps it's not as bad as it looks, he thought.

Archie made the decision. He closed his eyes and jumped.

Splash! The water closed over his head as he sank down, down, into the darkness. It was cold and murky. And it tasted HORRIBLE!

He struggled and kicked and flapped his tiny stumps of wings. Then, as he surfaced, he managed to grasp hold of some grass in his beak. Somehow he scrambled up on to the bank again. His lovely fluffy down was soaking and sticking to him.

Archie spluttered and shook himself to get the horrid, cold water off.

Father-duck was looking most disappointed in him. "I've never heard of a duck who can't swim," he said.

"Well, he hasn't exactly got the feet for it," said Mum.

They all looked down at Archie's feet. It was then that he noticed he hadn't got webbed feet like Mum or his brothers and sisters. He shivered miserably on the bank.

"Are you sure he's one of ours?" asked Father-duck. "We've never had one that looked like him before."

"Of course he is," said Mum. "His egg was in our nest. I watched him hatch out myself." She gave Archie a comforting glance. "I did notice he's a bit different – but he's really cute."

Some of the ducklings were swimming off, eager to explore. Mum spoke gently to Archie. "Will you be all right on your own for a bit, dear? I've got to help your father keep an eye on the others."

Archie nodded. "I – I suppose so."

"Go back up to the duck-house to keep warm," she told him. "Look, you can see it from here and I'll keep a watch out for you."

She jumped into the water and Archie gulped as all his family paddled off without him. He felt so alone.

Then Archie heard a noise and looked up to see the human called Jim. He wasn't riding the noisy machine now, he was walking towards the lake and he had a smaller human with him. "You've just got to see the ducklings, Poppy," Jim was saying.

Archie quickly scuttled back up to the duck-house. He didn't want to see anyone.

He stood inside, looking down at his feet and his long scaly toes. "Why am I different?" he wondered aloud.

Then he settled down in the nest to try to get warm. *Perhaps my webs will grow,* he thought hopefully. *Yes, that must be it. They just haven't grown yet – perhaps they're growing even now.* He cheered up a bit. *And perhaps when your webs have grown you actually want to jump into the water.*

Chapter 2

Poppy
"There's nothing to do round here."

"I'm not really interested in the ducks," said Poppy.

"But they're our first ducklings," said Jim, her father. "I saw them all marching down to the water when I was cutting the grass. There're ten of them and they're so cute."

Poppy was really fed up. She'd just had an email from her friend, Sophie, telling her what a great time she was having back where Poppy used to live.

Poppy wasn't having a good time at all. Her parents had taken over the landscape gardens three months ago and she hadn't made a single friend since they'd moved here. All the kids at her new school already had their friends and there were no other children living nearby.

"Look, there they go," said her father, as the ducklings, accompanied by their proud parents, swam into view. "Aren't they great?"

"They're OK, I suppose," said Poppy.

Her father sighed. "If you take an interest in things it might cheer you up a bit," he said. "I know your mother and I haven't been able to give you much attention lately. But once we're up and running we might be able to employ some staff, give us a bit of free time."

Poppy nodded and watched the ducklings paddling round and round.

The gardens had been part of the large eighteenth-century Deanswood Estate, which had been neglected for years.

Deanswood House had burnt down several years ago and now that part of the land had been sold off for redevelopment. An apartment block was being built on the land.

Poppy's parents had bought the gardens along with what had once been the gardener's cottage for them to live in. They were restoring the gardens with the intention of opening them to the public.

It's all right for them, thought Poppy. *They might be working hard, but at least they're doing what they want to do. I didn't want to come here. I'm not interested in plants and trees, or ducks and geese.* She gave a big sigh. *I really miss my old friends and there's absolutely nothing to do round here.*

"Oh look," cried her father. "The black swan cygnets have hatched too."

Poppy watched the five fluffy grey cygnets swimming obediently in a line between their elegant, watchful parents.

"That's wonderful," said her father. "We'll

soon have this lake alive with lots of water fowl, the way it must have been originally."

Poppy's gaze had wandered back to the ducklings. "I thought you said there were ten of them."

Her father frowned as he looked at them. "I'm sure I counted ten earlier. And there were definitely ten eggs in the nest."

They began looking for the missing duckling.

Poppy walked up to the duck-house and peered in through the door. "It's in here," she called, as she spotted Archie in the nest.

Her father came up to join her. "Why isn't it with the rest?"

"I don't know," said Poppy. "But it's a funny-looking duckling."

Her father peered in and gave a low chuckle. He beckoned Poppy away. "We don't want to frighten it," he whispered.

They walked quietly away from the

duck-house. "It's not a 'funny-looking duckling'," he explained. "It's a chick – a baby chicken."

"I didn't think we had any chickens."

"We haven't. Or at least we didn't have – up until now." He went on to explain that he'd been to the poultry breeder to look at the different breeds of ducks and geese. While he was there, they'd found an egg on its own quite near to the breeder's lake.

"Mr Pearce gave it to me and joked that I could take pot luck with it and use it to start off the restocking of my own lake," Poppy's father told her. "As our Aylesbury duck was already sitting on her own eggs, I sneaked the egg into her nest. She obviously didn't mind – or didn't notice – because she's hatched it!"

"But won't the chick be lonely on his own?" asked Poppy. She knew only too well what it felt like to be on your own.

"He'll be fine. I'll go and fetch a heat lamp to keep him warm when the ducks are out on the lake," he said. "And fortunately the weather's quite warm for the time of year. I'll get him some chick crumbs later."

He chuckled. "Mr Pearce has got several different breeds of chickens so goodness knows which kind this one is. We'll have to wait till he starts getting some feathers to see."

"It still seems unkind to keep him on his own," said Poppy.

"The mother duck will keep an eye out for him," said her father. "And she'll let him snuggle up to her at night with the ducklings. Plus he'll be something else for the visitors to look at when they come."

Poppy found herself going back to the duck-house later in the day. The heat lamp was on and it looked warm and cosy. Dad had already put the ducklings' first feed down but there was no sign of Archie.

Then she spotted him waiting on the bank of the lake. The mother duck was just leading her ducklings out of the water. Archie immediately joined in the line of ducklings as they marched back towards the duck-house.

She couldn't help smiling as she watched him. "Perhaps Dad's right – perhaps the little chick will be all right," she said to herself. "At least I hope he will be."

Chapter 3

Archie
Scratching the Earth

Archie's brothers and sisters were full of everything they'd seen and done on the lake. They eagerly told Archie all about it as they marched after their mother.

"We saw swans," Amanda told him.

"And geese," cheeped Aaron.

"And there were fish in the water," Angie giggled. "Swimming right underneath us."

"You've just got to join us," said Alec.

"I will," said Archie. "As soon as my webs grow."

Back at the duck-house, there were two

bowls outside and Mum explained it was their food and water. Archie went over to the water bowl for a drink while the others started on the food. He lifted his head and let the water trickle slowly down his throat. It certainly tasted better than the lake water.

As he moved to the food some of his brothers and sisters went over to the water bowl. He watched in horror as they plunged their beaks, full of food, into the water and "gargled" through it.

"Hey, you guys," he called. "You're making the water all mucky."

"Don't be silly, dear," said Mum. "Ducklings always eat like that. We like our food moist."

Archie tried some of the food – it tasted OK but he didn't fancy the water any more.

Then Jim arrived. He went straight up to Archie and put a small dish of food in front of him. "Here you are young-fellow-me-lad," he said. "This is just for you."

Archie wondered why he was getting special food. But it tasted good – and he only wished he had his own special water too.

After they'd all eaten, Mum called them into the duck-house. Jim closed the door after them and Mum explained it was to keep them safe in case any foxes came into the gardens at night.

Then she settled down on the nest and all the ducklings – and Archie – snuggled up under her soft feathers. Archie shut his eyes. The warmth made him sleepy and he felt happy and secure there with Mum and his brothers and sisters.

The next morning, Archie examined his feet for webs. They hadn't started growing yet but he remained quite cheerful. *Hey, they're bound to grow soon*, he thought.

More food and water was waiting for them when the duck-house door was opened to let them out. Archie made straight for the clean water before the others could get to it.

He had his own special dish of food again and this time it had some chopped greens in it as well. He really enjoyed those.

As soon as the others had finished their messy eating and drinking they formed a line behind Mum. "Today, I'm going to start showing you how to find good things to eat in the lake," said Mum.

Archie didn't follow them as they set off for the lake. He couldn't imagine anything that came out of that lake tasted good.

He was suddenly aware of a whirring sound above him. He looked up to see five large bluey-grey birds landing all around him.

Archie was startled. "Who are you? What do you want?"

"Who are we? Why, we're just a flock of friendly pigeons," said the largest one. "I'm Percy and that's Pauline, Paddy, Penny and Paul. And what do we want? Well, we've just come to see if there's any food left."

They all started pecking at the ground around the dishes where some food had been spilt.

"Don't you guys have any food of your own?" asked Archie.

"Food of our own?" said Penny, jerking her head back. "Well, we see it as all ours. We eat up anything that nobody else wants."

"Anything nobody else wants," repeated Paul. "Always good around the ducks – messy eaters."

Archie looked at their feet. They didn't have webs. "So you're not ducks then? You don't swim on the lake?"

Paddy looked up from his pecking. "Not ducks? Oh no, we're not ducks. We wouldn't want to swim on the lake."

"I'm a duck," said Archie. "But I can't swim either – at least not yet."

Pauline looked up and studied him with her beady eyes. "A duck? Can't swim? Are you sure you're a duck?"

"Of course I am. That's my mum down there. And all my brothers and sisters," said Archie. "Where do you live?"

"Where do we live?" said Paul. "We build our nests up high. In trees, on ledges of buildings, that sort of thing."

Archie looked up at the surrounding trees. He could see other birds up there, large black ones, small blue and yellow ones and a colourful black, white and red one that was pecking furiously at the tree trunk. They obviously weren't ducks either. Mum had never said anything about them sitting up in trees.

Then with a rush of wings, the pigeons took off again. "See you," called Percy.

"See you. See you," echoed the others.

Archie watched them go. He was alone again.

He started looking round where the pigeons had been pecking and spotted a piece of grain. "Hmm, that looks good." He pecked it up. Then he spotted another and pecked that up too.

He tried eating a small stone. "Ugh! Too hard," he decided, and left it.

Then Archie scratched the earth aside with his foot to see what else was there. He uncovered a tiny beetle. Surprised, Archie eyed it with first one eye and then the other. He jumped back as the beetle moved.

Then, with a decisive step forward, he quickly pecked it up.

"Mmm, nice," he said to himself. "This is fun." It felt good, the earth beneath his toes – it seemed natural somehow.

Archie scratched around a bit more, then he had a nap under the heat lamp.

When he woke up he decided to go and see if his brothers and sisters had finished their swimming on the lake. "I bet they'd like to try scratching around with me," he said.

He spotted them quite close to the bank. Mum had some muddy waterweed in her bill and was encouraging the ducklings to try it. That didn't look like fun at all.

Archie cheeped over to them. "Hey, come on guys, let's go peck around together," he called. "What say we scratch some earth – see what we can find?"

But nobody wanted to come and anyway, Mum said they had lots more to learn on the lake. "Why don't you sit and watch us, dear?" she suggested to Archie.

Archie miserably walked round the lake to a pile of rocks. The sun was shining on them and it was nice and warm. He found a small gap and went in and sat down to watch his brothers and sisters on the lake. He couldn't imagine ever wanting to go in the water – let alone search for muddy things to eat.

"Oh, there you are," said a voice. "I wondered where you'd got to."

He looked up to see Poppy. *Why did she wonder where I was?*

She sat down on a large rock next to him. "Poor little thing," she said. "I'm sure you must be lonely – no matter what Dad says."

She understood him. At least someone did. What a shame she wasn't a duck!

Chapter 4

Poppy
"We've got something in common."

Poppy settled down on the rock and thought about the email she'd just received. It was from her friend Ben this time. Like Sophie, he was full of plans for the Easter holidays and meeting up with the rest of the old gang.

"They're all having a great time," she said. "While I'm stuck here with nothing to do. It's so boring round here."

Archie looked up at her with his tiny head on one side.

"You know what?" she said to him.

"We've got something in common, you and me. Neither of us belongs here."

Poppy put her hand against her head. *I can't believe it*, she thought. *I'm sitting here talking to a bird – things must have really got to me!*

Archie let out a series of cheeps and she couldn't help smiling at him.

Then her mother arrived with a tray of plants and put them down at the water's edge. "These marsh marigolds are going to be a picture," she said to Poppy. "Look, some of them are coming out already – such a beautiful yellow."

Poppy nodded unenthusiastically. "Have you seen the latest arrival?" she asked, pointing to Archie.

"Oh, so that's him." Her mother chuckled. "Dad told me about him yesterday. Isn't he cute?"

"I'm sure he's lonely," said Poppy.

"He looks all right to me," said her

mother. "And this is a nice warm, sheltered spot. We'll all keep an eye out for him. Now I must get these planted." She kicked off her shoes and waded into the shallow water with the plants. "They'll look really nice just here by the rock feature."

Poppy looked up at the huge pile of rocks covered in greenery with wild primroses, cowslips and striking red campion growing in amongst them. Even the alder trees overlooking it from the other side of the fence, where Deanswood House had once stood, seemed extra tall and green.

Dad sometimes joked that it had been worth all the continuous rain they'd had to put up with at first to get such an attractive, green corner.

Poppy's mother finished her planting and stood up to admire her work. "I can't believe how much better this lake looks now," she said. "Do you remember how badly overgrown it was when we arrived?"

"Yes, I do," Poppy admitted. No one could deny that the whole gardens looked much better now. Mum and Dad had cleared the rubbish from the lake, cut back overgrown bushes and trees, cleared pathways and reshaped the lawns.

"We're just about on target for opening on Easter Sunday now," said her mother. "Another two weeks' hard work and we should be there."

"That's good," said Poppy, trying to sound enthusiastic. "Let's hope you don't get any more delays."

Unfortunately, the plans for the original eighteenth-century gardens had been destroyed in the house fire so Mum and Dad had spent hours researching what would have been growing there before planting anything new. That, along with the rain, had delayed the opening. They had originally planned to open a month ago.

"Did I tell you, we're planning an Easter egg hunt?" said Mum. "That should bring a few families in."

"It'll bring the little kids in," said Poppy. "What about people my age? Couldn't we have a disco or something?"

"I don't think that would be very suitable," said her mother, as she gathered up her shoes and tools. "Why don't you ask some of your new friends to come though? Perhaps we could have some games on the lawn."

"What new friends?" said Poppy quietly to herself, as her mother left. Even though she hated living there she didn't want her parents to know that she hadn't made any friends yet.

She was startled as Archie suddenly cheeped beside her. He was looking up at her.

"I bet you understand," she said to him. "You know what it's like not to have any mates, don't you?"

"Cheep, cheep," said Archie.

She banged the palm of her hand on her head again. *I'm doing it again*, she thought. *I'm talking to a bird!*

Poppy got out her book. She spent a lot

of her time reading, mainly about the adventures of Molly Mackenzie. Molly was very popular and never had trouble making friends. In the latest book she'd moved to a new school at the other end of the country and all the kids had been practically falling over themselves to make friends with her.

Nobody had fallen over themselves to make friends with Poppy. But she refused to let them see that it bothered her. On the school bus and every breaktime and lunchtime she sat reading. Molly Mackenzie's adventures were much more exciting than Poppy's life here.

Chapter 5

Archie
"Where do I fit in?"

The next morning, after breakfast, Archie followed his brothers and sisters down to the lake. He just knew that his webs would be growing very soon. *I ought to try and get used to being near the water for when they do,* he decided. *And at least if I'm on the bank, I'll be near to my family. Maybe I won't feel so lonely.*

After Mum and his brothers and sisters had paddled off to join Father-duck, Archie stared down into the water. "Why d'they all like the lake so much? It doesn't look very interesting to me. Yikes!" He jumped back as he realized there was a face staring back at him.

He slowly peered closer again and the face seemed to be coming towards him. Every time he moved, the face moved too. It was yellow and fluffy just like him. "It's me!" he cried.

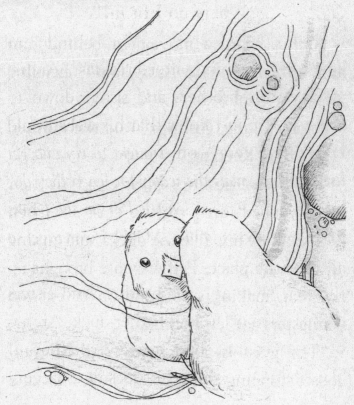

Fascinated, Archie studied his reflection in the water. Then he noticed something different about his face. His mouth was short and sharp whereas his brothers' and sisters' mouths were longer and more rounded.

He wasn't too concerned. "I expect that will change too when my webs grow," he said.

Archie heard a movement behind him and turned to see a goose family heading along the bank.

"Come along, goslings," said the mother. "Hup, hup. Keep up."

The twelve goslings quickly padded their little webbed feet over the grass after her. Not in a tidy line like the ducks but running all over the place. Father-goose brought up the rear, making sure none of his excited youngsters got left behind.

"The grass is good here," said Mother-goose, stopping abruptly and looking round her. The family immediately spread out and began eating the grass.

Archie was instantly interested. These birds had webbed feet but they weren't in the water. They were actually eating on the bank. He scurried over to them. "Hey, you guys. Mind if I peck around with you a while?"

"Yes, join us, join us," whistled the youngsters. "Be our friend, be our friend."

Archie joined in the middle of the goslings. He watched as they pulled at the grass with their beaks and copied them. The grass didn't taste too bad.

"What are you doing here all on your own, sweetie?" Mother-goose asked Archie.

"My family are out on the lake," Archie told her. He wondered if there was anything tasty down amongst the grass roots and started scratching with his feet. Several ants ran out. "Hey, they look good to eat," said Archie, remembering the tiny beetle he'd eaten yesterday.

"Ugh!" said one gosling.

"Disgusting," whistled another.

"We're vegetarians," explained Father-goose. "We don't eat meat."

"Oh, OK," said Archie. He didn't want to upset his new friends. If it meant just eating grass, then that's what he'd do – even if it did get a bit boring after a while.

All was quiet and peaceful around the lake; the only thing to be heard was the gentle sound of the geese pulling at the grass. Archie felt happy.

Then he heard a flapping sound above him and looked up. It wasn't the pigeons this time, but two Mallard ducks. Archie watched them fly over the lake and skid to a halt on the surface of the water.

"Wow!" cried Archie. "That's so clever."

"Not really," said Mother-goose. "All ducks, geese and swans can fly."

Archie was so excited. "Oh, I can't wait till I can fly." He immediately imagined himself flying way up high above everything.

"I'm afraid you won't be able to fly as well as that, sweetie," said Mother-goose. "You'll be able to fly a bit when you're older, but not as well as that."

"Why not? You said all ducks can fly – and I'm a duckling."

"Oh dear me, you're not a duckling," said Mother-goose.

"Yes, I am – that's my Mother- and Father-duck over there on the lake," said Archie indignantly. "And my brothers and sisters – we all hatched out together. Mum did say I'm a bit different – but she said I'm cute."

"Oh you're different all right, sweetie," said Mother-goose. "You're a chick – a baby chicken."

"But – how do you know?"

Father-goose stepped forward. "We know because we fly around quite a bit, visit lots of places. We often see ducks and chickens and believe me, you're definitely a chick."

The goslings had stopped eating now and were all watching him. Some of them had bits of grass sticking out of their bills.

"Is – is that why I can't swim?"

"Chickens don't swim," said Father-goose.

"Not even if my webs grow?"

"Chickens don't have webbed feet, sweetie," said Mother-goose. "And you must have noticed you've got a beak instead of a bill. Chickens like to peck around a lot, not scoop up food and water like ducks do."

"But my mum—"

"Your mum will be your foster-mum," said Mother-goose gently. "And I'm sure she loves you and will take care of you."

"We've got to go now," said Father-goose. "Come on, goslings. Hup, hup. Down to the lake for your baths. Then you can have a good swim."

The goslings all padded off with their

parents and Archie was left devastated. So he was a chick – a baby chicken. His mind was whirring with questions. *What's a chicken? What'll I look like when I grow up?* he wondered. *Are there other chickens here? And how come I hatched out in a duck's nest?*

Archie felt more lonely than ever. He retreated to the rock feature and crept into his warm little hidey-hole amongst the rocks. He sat down and watched over the lake. There were several different kinds of birds there but none of them could be chickens because they were all swimming. Father-goose said that chickens didn't swim.

The lonely little chick watched the goslings with their parents, the black swan cygnets with theirs and the ducklings…

"Where do I fit in?" Archie wondered miserably.

Chapter 6

Poppy
Decisions

Poppy was getting more worried about Archie. Every day when she came home from school she looked for him. And every time she found him he was in a different place.

One day he had been following a moorhen as it strutted across the grass. When the moorhen had plopped into the lake Archie had just stared after it looking so disappointed. Another day he was looking up into the trees at a family of rooks. Then on Wednesday, Poppy had found him being chased away from the white swan's nest by a very irate male swan. Now he was sitting watching a coot's nest in the reeds.

"I'm sure he knows he's different," she'd told Dad yesterday. "He's trying to find out where he belongs."

"Chickens aren't that intelligent," said Dad. "He's got his heat lamp for when it gets chilly and plenty of food. And he's still snuggling up to the female duck at night, so he'll be all right."

Poppy hadn't agreed but it was no use arguing with Dad. He was pretty uptight at the moment about getting everything ready for the opening on Easter Sunday.

She slung her schoolbag down by the lake. *Thank goodness school's broken up for the Easter holiday now*, she thought. She was so relieved not to have to go back for two whole weeks.

"Two weeks when I won't have to pretend

that I don't mind being ignored by the other children," she said aloud. She'd read all her Molly Mackenzie books several times now but there was a new one coming out next week. Mum had promised to get it for her.

Poppy sighed. "My only hope is that Mum and Dad will get fed up with it here. Then we can go home." (She could never think of this place as her home.)

She turned as she heard a quacking. The Aylesbury duck was heading up the bank with her ducklings in tow. She was looking all around her and calling.

"I bet you're looking for your little foster-chick, aren't you?" said Poppy.

Archie appeared, out of the reeds, running towards her. He joined in with the row of ducklings as they marched up to the duck-house. Poppy noticed that Archie, as well as the ducklings, now had fluffy white wing feathers appearing through their yellow down.

Then she heard her own mother shouting from the house. "Poppy! Poppy, get in here quick."

It sounded urgent so Poppy grabbed her schoolbag and ran as fast as she could.

"It's your father," her mother told her. "He's had an accident. He was cutting back that big pine tree and he slipped and fell."

"Oh no," cried Poppy. "Is he all right?"

"I think he's broken his leg," said Mum tearfully. "I've just phoned for an ambulance."

It was the following day before Dad was allowed home from hospital. He'd broken his left leg badly in two places and they'd had to operate on it. He'd also broken his left arm so he'd be out of action for some time.

The hospital had loaned Dad a wheelchair and Mum pushed him into the lounge. Poppy went in to see him but Mum was kneeling next to him holding his hand. They were so deep in conversation that they didn't seem to notice her.

"I'll manage somehow," her mother was saying.

"You can't possibly do all that work on your own by Easter," said Dad. "It's only a week away. This is the final straw. First all that rain held us up, then there was all the research we had to do because we didn't have the original plans."

"But we've worked so hard," said Mum. "We can't just give up. This place – it was our dream."

"If we'd been able to open a month ago, as we'd hoped, things might have been different," said Dad. "But now we've run out of money. We've got bills mounting up all over the place." His voice started to shake as he continued. "Without the paying public coming in we're finished."

"We could just open anyway," suggested Mum. "The posters and all the advertising have already gone out."

"The gardens aren't good enough yet,"

said Dad. "There's all those weeds for a start. People will be asking for their money back. And they certainly won't come again." He gave a big sigh that was almost a sob. "I've had a Mr Parker badgering me to sell to him recently. Better to cut our losses and sell up."

Poppy's mother started crying and Poppy didn't know what to think. She didn't want to stay here – she'd never wanted to come in the first place. Now it looked as though they might be leaving…

She tiptoed out and went up to her room to think. She couldn't bear seeing her parents so upset. *I guess I'd never realized quite what it meant to them before*, she thought.

Poppy went and looked out of the window at the gardens and the lake. "Only yesterday I was hoping they'd get fed up with it here and we could go back to our old town," she said to herself. "But they haven't had a chance to enjoy it yet, let alone get fed up with it. All they've had so far is three months' really hard work and one problem after another."

She thought of their tired, tear-stained faces and suddenly she knew what she had to do.

Chapter 7

Archie
"I think you might be my mum."

Archie was sure he'd found a chicken this time. He'd investigated just about every bird he'd seen. Some had been nice to him and felt sorry for him but others had shouted at him to get away from their nest and even chased him, like the huge white swan.

But this bird was a chicken – he just knew it was. It didn't have webbed feet and it had a beak. All right, so maybe its beak was longer than his beak, but Archie's would grow. And so would his legs and neck, then one day Archie would be just as tall, just as elegant.

The chicken was standing in the shallow water by the rocks so it obviously lived here. It all added up. Was it his mum or his dad?

"Excuse me," said Archie.

The chicken remained motionless, its beady eyes fixed staring into the water. "Shh. You'll disturb the fish. I've already missed one."

"But I think you might be my mum."

The tall bird swung its head round to look at him. "Why, it's a little chick. Mmm." It snapped its long beak a couple of times as it turned and slowly started to wade through the water towards him. "Yes, I'm your mum. Come to mummy, little chick."

Archie's heart leapt.

But then suddenly Poppy appeared, running towards them and waving a huge fork in the air. She shouted at the chicken. "Get away from him!"

Startled, the tall bird opened its huge wings and took off. It rose majestically into the air, flapping its wings with its long legs trailing behind it.

Archie was devastated. *Why did she do that? She's frightened off my mum.*

"That was a heron," Poppy told Archie. "You must watch out for them, Little Chick. Dad's told me all about herons. They eat lots of fish but they also sometimes eat frogs, ducklings and small birds – like you."

Archie shuddered. So it wasn't his mum. The heron had pretended it was so it could … eat him! He gulped.

There just wasn't a chicken here – anywhere. He would probably never meet his mum. Mother-duck was kind to him and she even said it didn't matter him being a chick, she still loved him. But she and the ducklings were always on the lake. Archie still spent most of his time alone. That was obviously how it was always going to be.

The lonely little chick dejectedly followed Poppy as she walked over to a large patch of undergrowth. "I'm very busy today," she told Archie. "Dad's broken his leg, and his arm, and I've offered to help get this place ready for opening at Easter. Mum and I are going to be incredibly busy all week."

Archie watched as she dug the big fork into the ground. "This is supposed to be a flower bed, would you believe?" she said. "At least I don't have to worry about what's weeds and what isn't here – Mum says it's all weeds. So I can just dig it all up."

Archie didn't understand everything she was talking about – but it was just so nice that someone wanted to stay and talk to him.

"Mum's got some summer bulbs to go in here, and some new bushes," she said. She pulled out a bunch of weeds and threw them into a wheelbarrow.

Archie sat down to watch. Then, as Poppy tugged at a particularly large weed, seeds shook out all over the grass. *Yum, they look tasty*, thought Archie. He jumped up and started to peck up the seeds.

Poppy chuckled. "That's really helpful, Little Chick. If you eat all the seeds they can't grow into more weeds."

Archie felt happy that she was pleased with him. He moved closer to watch for more seeds falling. Then, as Poppy dug over some earth, his eye caught a movement. It was another tiny beetle. He looked up at Poppy. Did she want it?

Poppy wasn't taking any notice of it. *If she's not quick it'll be gone*, he thought.

Archie had to make a decision. He darted forward and pecked it up. Then he looked up at Poppy. *I hope she won't be cross with me for eating her beetle*, he thought. *Or maybe she'll be upset with me because she's a vegetarian like the geese.*

But she smiled at him and he felt a warmth creep right through him.

After that he kept alongside her. Sometimes he jumped back when a huge beetle was uncovered or a large earthworm, but there were lots of tiny creatures too. Poppy obviously didn't want any of the seeds or the bugs she scratched up with her fork.

Archie couldn't see her feet as she kept them covered but he guessed she hadn't got claws. *That must be why she has to use a fork*, he decided.

When Poppy stopped for a rest, Archie started scratching at the earth himself. Poppy sat back on the grass watching him. "You're managing so well on your own," she said to him. "Especially since you've not had your real mother to teach you. You're still so tiny but you seem to know what to do."

Archie decided that Poppy was nice. Even though she wasn't a chicken, he liked her.

After Poppy had finished scratching up the earth, she brought him his midday dish of chick crumb mix. But he was so full he could hardly eat any of it.

He had a little sleep in his warm hidey-hole in the rocks while Poppy went off for her lunch.

Poppy came back later with her mother. They were carrying large boxes with holes in the lids and they put them down on the grass by the lake.

Archie ran over to investigate. He got excited as he heard scuffling noises coming from the boxes. *Poppy's brought me some chickens*, he thought. *She said she knew I was lonely.*

But as she opened the first box his hopes were immediately dashed. "Did you say these are Mandarin ducks?" Poppy asked her mother.

Her mother nodded and carefully lifted out the first duck. Its feathers were the most beautiful colours Archie had ever seen. "There's two pairs of Mandarins," she said, taking the other three out of the box. The two brightly coloured males and the two paler females walked straight to the water's edge and jumped in.

"Then these other ducks are the Pochards," she said opening the second box. "And the pair of Wigeons. The Egyptian geese should be coming tomorrow."

No chickens then, thought Archie, disappointed. *I'm still on my own.*

Chapter 8

Poppy
Hard Work

Poppy was exhausted. She just wasn't used to all this hard work. But she had to keep going. Whenever she felt like giving up she just pictured her parents' tired, tear-stained faces.

Mum and Dad had been so surprised and grateful when she'd offered to help. Although she'd actually had to persuade Dad she could do it. That she and Mum really could get the gardens ready for opening at Easter.

He'd eventually decided to let them try.

"Even if we do sell up we won't get the money straight away," he'd decided. "So I guess waiting one more week won't make much difference."

"We can always live off all those Easter eggs we've bought for the Easter egg hunt if it doesn't work out," Mum had joked.

Mum had just finished cutting back all the roses along the rose walk and Poppy was weeding round them. Archie was at her feet as usual.

"I still can't believe I'm doing all this when all I want to do is leave here and go back to our old home," she said to him. Then she laughed as Archie dived after a centipede. He looked so disappointed when it got away. "At least you always manage to cheer me up."

"Cheep," said Archie. He was getting bigger and more fluffy white feathers were growing out of his baby down. The ducklings also had lots of lovely white feathers now.

Mum had moved on to trimming the ornamental hedges. Dad had spent days cutting them back and reshaping them when they'd first arrived. They were looking good now.

"Right, that's enough weeding for today," said Poppy, standing up and straightening her aching back. "Time to move on to washing off the statues by the lake."

"Cheep, cheep," said Archie.

"All right, I promise not to splash you like I did when I was scrubbing the steps to the terrace," she chuckled. "I didn't know you'd followed me up there. I wouldn't have shaken the brush if I'd known you were standing behind me."

"Cheep," said Archie.

Poppy picked him up and put him on top of the wheelbarrow full of weeds. He sat there happily as she pushed it along the path lined with large, green-leaved rhododendrons.

"Dad says these rhododendrons will be coming into bloom soon, and they'll be really spectacular," she told Archie. "I like those smaller red ones that are already flowering by the lake. The colours all reflect in the water."

"Cheep, cheep," said Archie.

Poppy was getting used to having him around. She no longer felt strange "talking to a bird". It seemed natural somehow. And anyway, Archie wasn't "just a bird" – he was a real little character.

The statues looked really good when she'd finished. With all the dirt and grime washed off them you could clearly see the details. Then it suddenly started to rain heavily – huge drops quickly followed by thunder and lightning. Poppy gathered up her things and the Aylesbury duck appeared to usher her brood, including Archie, to the safety of the duck-house.

Poppy raced back to the cottage and was followed in by her mother.

"I can't believe this," said Mum, shaking out her wet hair. "I was intending to start on the lawns this evening. This is really going to hold us up."

"It might not last long," said Poppy hopefully.

"The weather forecast is quite good for the next couple of days," said Dad. "But we'll still have to wait for the grass to dry off a bit before Mum can start on it. I'm afraid we're running out of time."

"I could help with it," said Poppy.

"You can't drive the motor mower," said Mum. "And anyway, we need you to finish the weeding and then plant all those new climbing plants we bought to cover the fence behind the rock feature."

"If only there was some way I could help,"

said Dad. "I just can't see us getting ready on time. It's just one thing after another—"

He broke off as the doorbell rang.

Mum went to answer it and returned with Mr Dixon, the man who had bought the site next door where Deanswood House had stood.

Poppy liked Mr Dixon. He was always cheerful and he'd been straight round with a huge box of chocolates when he'd heard about Dad's accident. He had retired from his job as a fire fighter recently and he'd told them he was developing the site next door to keep himself out of mischief!

"I've come to ask for your advice, Jim," Mr Dixon said to Dad. "The apartment building is well under way now so I've started to think about the communal gardens."

He went on to explain that he'd like to keep the gardens as traditional as possible, but at the same time easy to care for. "As I'm going to be living in one of the apartments I thought I'd have a go at keeping them up myself," he said. "I don't know much about gardening but I'm keen to learn."

"Good idea," said Dad. "So you'd like my advice about the sort of plants and shrubs to use?"

Mr Dixon nodded. "Yes please, and any other advice you can give me."

"Have you had a chance to look at what the soil's like?" asked Dad.

"Well, I've started doing battle with the undergrowth," said Mr Dixon. "One area seems to have a lot of clay and there's obviously a drainage problem at the far end – no doubt after all the rain we've had. The ground's rather boggy, but a bit of pipe-work will soon sort that. Otherwise it looks pretty good."

Poppy had been listening and an idea was rapidly forming in her mind. "Excuse me, Mr Dixon," she said politely. "But you said

you're really keen to learn about gardening?"

"Sure am," said Mr Dixon. "Always ready for a challenge, that's me."

"Well, I wondered if you'd consider giving us a hand?" asked Poppy. "As you know, Dad can't do anything now – and Mum and I are running out of time, particularly with the lawns. We're opening on Sunday."

"Poppy," said Dad, obviously embarrassed. "That's cheeky – and rude. Mr Dixon's got his own business to sort out."

"No, wait a minute," said Mr Dixon. "She's got every right to ask for my help. After all, I'm asking for yours."

"But we can't afford to pay anyone for help," said Mum.

"Who said anything about paying?" said Mr Dixon. "If you help me out with advice then the least I can do is help you. Plus the experience will be good for me – and I'm really keen to try out a motor mower."

"That would be fantastic," said Dad. "I could even do a garden design for you if you like. At least I can use my right hand."

"Great," said Mr Dixon. He turned and smiled at Poppy. "We've got a deal, young lady. I'll be round tomorrow to get my instructions."

Mum and Dad were looking hopeful again. Poppy even found herself feeling quite excited.

Chapter 9

Archie
Easter Eggs

Archie put his head on one side. He wondered what the strange sound was.

Then Poppy arrived carrying a box. "Are you listening to the church bells, Little Chick?" she asked him. "It's Easter Sunday. And we're actually ready for our first visitors – at last. We're opening today."

Archie's attention was drawn to the box. *More ducks?* he wondered. *Or could it be – chickens?* He hardly dared hope.

Poppy put the box down on the ground and opened the lid. "I've just got to hide these Easter eggs before the visitors arrive," she told him.

Archie was immediately interested. *Eggs! Could Easters be a type of chicken?* He looked up at Poppy.

Poppy picked him up. "D'you want to see them, Little Chick?" She held him up to look in the box.

Archie's little heart leapt as he peered in. *Beautiful shiny eggs!*

Poppy smiled at him. "They're pretty, aren't they? D'you like them?"

They ARE chickens! Poppy's got them for me so I'll have some friends, he thought. *And she's going to hide them away from these visitors she keeps talking about.*

Archie was so excited. Poppy was kind to him. He loved her, he really did. But it would be great to have some chickens around too.

Poppy put him down again and gathered up several of the eggs. Archie followed her as she walked over to a hedge. She carefully placed a silver egg under it. Then she put a green one under a weeping willow tree and a red one under the huge oak. A shiny gold egg went under the camellia and a blue one behind the cedar of Lebanon tree.

He was puzzled as he followed Poppy back to the box for more eggs and then as she hid them under more trees and bushes. *Why isn't she putting the eggs in a nest?* he wondered. *Perhaps chickens don't have nests. But who's going to keep them warm?* Archie knew that eggs have to be kept warm to hatch them out. *There's certainly no chickens here to sit on them,* he thought.

Except me, of course. But I can't keep them all warm on my own.

Poppy had just put a very pretty silver and blue egg behind a statue of a cherub. "I think this is the prettiest one," she said. "What do you think, Little Chick?"

So that was it, he was supposed to choose.

Poppy thought this was the best one – and so did he. *This is the one I'll hatch out*, Archie decided.

He did wonder briefly why Poppy was still putting so many more out, but quickly forgot about the others as he examined his egg. It was a very pretty silver and blue and a perfect egg shape. It was almost the same size as him so it wasn't going to be easy.

Archie hopped up on to the egg. But it immediately rolled away and he fell off. He tried again. This time he managed to balance for a full two seconds before he fell off.

He rolled the egg back with his beak and jumped up again. He fell off and rolled along the ground a little way himself that time. Archie scrabbled to his feet and shook his feathers. He wasn't going to give up.

He looked at the ground next to the statue. *If I could just wedge the egg between that clump of grass and the statue it might stop it rolling*, he thought. He rolled the egg a little way with his beak. Then he stood on one leg and pushed it with the other. Little by little the egg moved into place.

Archie jumped on again and this time he stayed there. He happily settled down. He was just so excited – he was going to have a brother or a sister. He really didn't mind which.

"I hope I'm keeping you warm enough," he cheeped to the egg. He wriggled a bit and tried opening his tiny wings to cover a little more. "I'm going to keep you warm until you hatch."

The happy little chick started imagining what he would say to him or her when they hatched. "I can show them all round the gardens," he said to himself. "I'll introduce them to Poppy and to Mother-duck and the ducklings. And to the geese and the black swan cygnets. And I'll be sure to tell them not to jump in the lake."

Archie felt warm and happy. He had no idea how long he would have to sit there. But he didn't mind – he'd stay there as long as he had to. He started to doze off and began to dream about having a brother or sister. And maybe later, he'd be able to hatch one or two of the other eggs…

Archie was woken up suddenly by lots of

shouts and laughter. He looked up to see several children running into the gardens carrying baskets. He went cold as he watched them gathering up the Easter eggs. "What are they doing? They're stealing my eggs!"

Archie panicked. This just couldn't be happening. "Eeek! Eeek," he screeched, as loud as he could to alert Poppy. But he couldn't see her anywhere.

Suddenly a little girl spotted him. "Oh look!" she cried. "One of the Easter eggs has hatched out!"

Silly thing, thought Archie. *Of course it hasn't hatched out yet. I'm just keeping it warm.*

But in a flash the little girl had scooped both him and the egg up and popped them into her basket.

Chapter 10

Poppy
Ups and Downs

Poppy heard Archie's terrified screeching and ran to find him. She was just in time to see his stricken face peeping out of a little girl's basket.

"Wait," she cried, running over to her.

Poppy reached the little girl just at the same time as a boy about her own age did. "You can't take him," she told the girl.

"What's my sister done now?" asked the boy.

"She's got our chick in her basket," Poppy told him.

The boy laughed as he spotted Archie. "Where'd you get that, Katy?" he asked the little girl.

"He's hatched out of an egg," she said indignantly. "I found him, so he's mine."

"No, he's not," said the boy, carefully lifting Archie out of the basket and handing him to Poppy. "You've got your eggs. Chicks weren't included in the price."

"Humph!" said Katy, stamping away.

Poppy put Archie down and watched him scuttle away under a bush. She laughed, relieved. "Thanks," she said to the boy.

"S'OK," he said. "I'm Toby, I've seen you at school."

"Oh," said Poppy. She hadn't recognized him. But then she hadn't paid much attention to the unfriendly children.

"Makes a change to see you without your head in a book," said Toby.

"Sorry?"

"You're always reading," said Toby. "We all wondered why you didn't want to make friends with anyone."

"What?" Poppy couldn't believe what she was hearing. "But I was desperate to make friends. I was only reading because I thought no one wanted to talk to me."

Toby laughed. "We all thought you were stuck-up – didn't want to know any of us."

Poppy laughed too. "I can't believe it!"

"I'll introduce you to everyone next term," said Toby. "They're all right, in our class – well most of them anyway." He went on to tell her about each member of the class.

Poppy was fascinated and Toby was so funny the way he described some of the children. None of them sounded a bit like she'd imagined. They all sounded much nicer.

They began to walk round the grounds together. Every now and again Poppy spotted Archie running from under one bush to another. Or from behind a tree to a hedge. He was no doubt keeping out of the way of more children.

"You're lucky living here – it's cool," said Toby. "My dad's been wanting to get a proper look in here for ages. He's really keen on local history you see. And he's got me interested too now."

"I don't know much about the gardens," said Poppy. She paused and thought about it. "At least I didn't…"

"But this place is special," said Toby. "Part of the history of this area."

"I'd never thought of it like that before," said Poppy. "I hated it here, at first. I missed my mates. I missed the shops, the cinemas, bowling alleys, that sort of thing."

"But there's things to do round here too," said Toby. "There's some great after-school clubs. If you hadn't been so—"

"I know – stuck-up," Poppy said, laughing.

Toby laughed too. "Y'know, your mum and dad have done a fantastic job. These gardens look brilliant now and they're just like they must have looked in the eighteenth century."

"Several of the trees and bushes are the originals," said Poppy. "And most of the hedges."

"See, you do know something." Toby gave her a friendly shove.

"Well, I've been helping out a bit." Poppy smiled. "And I've even quite enjoyed it."

"The lake's great with all the ducklings and the baby geese and swans," said Toby. "D'you get to look after them?"

"I do now, since Dad's accident," said Poppy. She chuckled. "I didn't want to at first. I didn't particularly like ducks and geese. But once you get to know them, well, you find they're really cute."

"Cool," said Toby. "What about the chick?"

"Oh, he's special," said Poppy with a smile. "He's such a character."

By closing time, Poppy and Toby were still talking. Toby's father, with Katy in tow, came to find him to go home. Toby introduced him to Poppy.

"Quite a place you've got here, Poppy," said Toby's father. "I'd love to meet your parents, have a chat with them."

Poppy thought that was a good idea. So she led the way over to the terrace where Poppy's mum had laid out the tables and chairs for tea for the visitors. Dad was sitting at a table in his wheelchair counting the takings.

He was talking to Mum as they approached. "I think we've taken just enough to cover the bills," he said. "Things are going to be tight but if we can carry on like this, it might just work."

He looked up and smiled at them and

Poppy introduced everyone. They all shook hands and Mum scurried off to fetch tea and cake.

The two fathers got on immediately and were soon deep in conversation. Katy had put her basket under the table and sat on a chair eating one of her Easter eggs.

Poppy and Toby went to help carry the tea things just as Archie shot out from under a hedge and disappeared behind a tree.

"Does he always dash about like that?" asked Toby.

"No, I think he must be excited at all the company today," said Poppy.

They got back just in time to hear Toby's father ask: "How have you managed to overcome the problem of the lake almost drying up every summer?"

"What?" said Poppy's father, obviously shocked. "I wasn't aware there was a problem. It's been full as long as we've been here."

"Well, we have had a lot of rain lately," said Toby's father. He went on to tell him that because he'd been interested in the place, he'd often peeped over the outer fences. That was when he'd spotted the water level dropped in the summer. "I've noticed it over a few years," he told him. "It tends to fill up again during the autumn and winter."

"But I was led to believe that it was a natural lake," said Dad, going decidedly pale. "I assumed there was an underground spring."

"The lake – and the water-fowl – are the main attraction," said Mum, slumping down into a chair. "People won't be so keen to come without it. We won't take the money we need to keep running."

"It never occurred to me that I needed to get the water supply checked out," said Dad. "How stupid of me! But this place was exactly what we've always dreampt of owning – and there were a couple of other people interested in it. We had to move fast."

Mum put her head in her hands. She looked devastated.

Dad explained to Toby's father how they'd sunk every penny they had into the gardens. It would cost a fortune to fill the lake from the metered water supply. And that would only be if they could get permission, which was extremely unlikely.

"I'm so sorry," said Toby's father. "I had no idea you didn't know. I've totally spoilt your day."

"No, I'm grateful to you," said Dad. "At least now we can get out before we sink any more money into it."

Chapter 11

Archie
The Rock Feature

Archie was exhausted. He'd been frantically searching for his eggs all afternoon. He'd looked under the bushes and hedges and behind all the trees where he remembered Poppy had hidden them, but they were all gone. The children had stolen every one of them.

He spotted Poppy sitting with others at one of the tables. He shuffled slowly and dejectedly towards her but she didn't notice him. She was too busy talking to her new friend – Toby.

In fact everyone at the table seemed to be busy talking. Then he noticed the basket under the table – it had HIS egg in it. The silver and blue one he'd been trying to hatch.

Archie rushed up to it, jumped straight into the basket and settled down on his egg. This was comfy and much easier to sit on in the basket. He snuggled in but he could hear Poppy talking. She sounded upset.

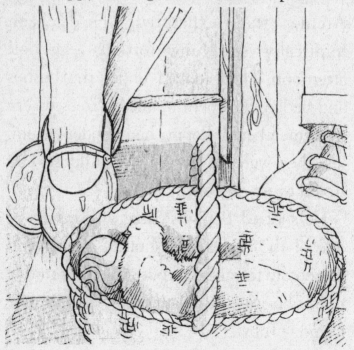

"But I like living here now. I've actually enjoyed working in the grounds – and having Little Chick around," she said. "And I'm even looking forward to going back to school now that I've met Toby. I don't want to leave here."

Archie sat up again. Poppy was talking about leaving. Where was she going?

"I can't see any choice but to sell up," said Dad. "This really is the final straw. The lake – or what's left of it – will probably smell in the summer and we won't be able to keep the ducks and geese. We'll never make this place pay now."

Archie could hear someone crying.

"I wish there was something I could do to help," said another voice.

"And what about Little Chick?" asked Poppy. "We can't just leave him here."

Archie began to panic. *What does she mean, leave me here? Isn't she coming back?*

Then Katy reached under the table and grabbed the basket without looking. Archie was tipped out on to the grass.

Just as he scrabbled to his feet he heard Poppy's mother say: "I just can't believe it. After all our dreams, all our hard work – we've got to leave it all behind."

Archie was heartbroken. They were leaving – all of them. And they were leaving everything behind. That would include him. Now his last egg had gone too. "I'll be all on my own," he gasped. He'd never felt so miserable. Never felt so lonely.

Archie ran off towards the lake to find Mother-duck and the ducklings. But he couldn't see them, so he climbed up the grassy bank to the top of the rock feature. Maybe he could see them from there. He spotted them right on the other side of the lake, but they didn't hear him when he called to them. They were too busy practising bobbing upside down to search for food.

Archie started to climb down to his hidey-hole but he slipped. He frantically tried to grasp at the rocks but they were too big for his tiny feet to grip. He slithered right down into a small gap.

Then he was falling into the darkness and he landed on a ledge. Fortunately it was covered in thick moss so he didn't hurt himself. But he couldn't see a way out. It was dark and it was damp – it was HORRIBLE! And he couldn't see any way he could ever get out again.

"Eeek!" he screeched. "Eeek, eeek, eeeeeek!"

No one will hear me, he thought miserably. *No one will come looking for me. They don't care about me – they're all going off and leaving me.*

Archie didn't know how long he'd been down there, but it felt like hours before he heard Poppy's voice.

"I bet he's gone to his hidey-hole," she said.

"It's over here, in the rock feature."

"He was certainly heading this way," said Toby. "He just shot out from under the table and took off."

"Little Chick. Little Chick," called Poppy. "Where are you?"

Archie screeched again.

Poppy's voice was closer now. "He is here. I can hear him. But he's not in his usual place."

Then Archie could hear them above him. "Cheep, cheep," he shouted.

"It sounds as though he's inside the rock feature," said Toby.

"But how could he be?" said Poppy. "Wait a minute, there's a gap in the rocks here. He could have fallen through it."

"We'll have to pull off some of the plants and grass," said Toby. "Then we'll see if we can move one or two of the rocks. D'you think your dad'll mind?"

"No," said Poppy. "Especially now we've got to sell up. But in any case we've got to get Little Chick."

Archie could hear tearing noises and then a scraping sound directly above him. He screeched in terror.

"Careful! Careful, with the rocks," cried Poppy. "We mustn't hurt him. He's so tiny and delicate." She sounded as though she was crying.

"Don't worry, I'll be really careful," said Toby. "There's quite a big gap down there."

A shaft of sunlight suddenly flooded in to Archie as the rock immediately above him was removed.

"I can see him," said Toby. "He looks OK but he's quite a way down. I think we'd better get off the top here before we take away any more rocks. With that large hole there it could all collapse."

Archie heard them scrambling down and then more rocks were removed. A pair of hands reached in and picked him up. He was passed gently out to Poppy.

"Oh, Little Chick, you're all right," cried Poppy.

"Cheep, cheep," said Archie. He was so happy to be out again and especially to see Poppy.

Toby was still removing rocks. "You know

what I think?" he said. He was looking excited. "I don't think this was originally a rock feature at all."

"It wasn't?" said Poppy.

"No, I bet anything it was a grotto," said Toby. "And some time ago it collapsed."

"What's a grotto?" asked Poppy.

"It's a sort of picturesque cave," said Toby. "Often an artificial cave – lots of eighteenth-century gardens had them. They were very fashionable, according to my dad. He loves this sort of thing."

"D'you think he could tell us about this one?" asked Poppy.

"Sure," said Toby. "I'll go and get him."

As he ran off, Poppy looked at Archie who was still sitting in her hands. "What have you discovered, Little Chick?"

Chapter 12

Poppy
"No wonder this area is so green."

Poppy was curious about the possible grotto. She carefully put Archie down on the ground and climbed over some of the rocks.

With the outer rocks and some of the vegetation removed she could see there were large gaps here and there. The rocks were all higgledy-piggledy, not in any order or design. "It's got to be something that's collapsed," she said.

She looked round at Archie. "It was very lucky you didn't get hurt, falling all that way. Some of these rocks look quite sharp."

"Cheep," said Archie. He started cleaning up his white feathers with his beak.

Poppy put her hand in and ran it round one or two of the rocks. "Ah, there's some nice soft moss in here, that's probably what saved you. But how would moss be growing in here?"

Poppy peered further into the rocks and, as her eyes became accustomed to the darkness, she could see something glistening. She put her hand in again. "It's water. It's really wet in here!"

"Cheep, cheep," said Archie.

She looked up to the greenery covering the rocks and the surrounding banks. She remembered Dad mentioning that everything grew particularly well in this corner.

"One thing I've learnt about gardening is that plants need water," she said. "With all the water in the rocks, no wonder this area is so green."

Toby arrived back then. "Our dads, both of them, will be here in a minute. They're just looking at some paperwork."

Poppy quickly told him about the water and the greenery.

"Where's the water coming from?" asked Toby, peering into the rocks.

"Well it can't be coming from the lake, it's too far back," said Poppy. "D'you think it could be a spring?"

"Could be," said Toby. "But where is the spring? And why isn't the water bubbling out?"

"Dad said he'd thought there was a natural underground source for the lake," said Poppy. "But with the lake almost drying up every summer we know there can't be."

"This must be something quite independent of the lake," said Toby. "If this is a spring it could be blocked."

"Like by the rocks when the grotto collapsed?" said Poppy.

"But then the water would have had to go somewhere," said Toby. "A spring doesn't stop flowing just because it's blocked. The whole of this surrounding area would be wet. And it's not."

Poppy looked up at the alder trees on the other side of the boundary fence. Dad admired them as they were so tall and so green. "I've just remembered something," she said. "The other night Mr Dixon, who's developing the site where Deanswood House was, mentioned he had a drainage problem on part of the land. I wonder…"

She climbed over the grassy bank next to the rock feature, to the fence immediately behind it. She pulled herself up on the fence, carefully avoiding the new plants, and peered over. "Come and look," she called.

Toby scrambled over too and Archie followed him.

"It's really wet over here," said Poppy breathlessly. "Quite boggy by the looks of it. This must be the area Mr Dixon meant."

"So it could be a blocked spring," said Toby. "And maybe it's not independent of the lake at all –"

"Maybe it originally fed the lake," Poppy finished for him.

Archie seemed to have picked up on the excitement. "Cheep, cheep," he joined in.

They rushed back as they heard their fathers coming. Toby's father was pushing Dad over in his wheelchair. "Don't say anything about the possible spring yet," whispered Poppy. "Let's see what your father thinks first."

Toby's father immediately started examining the rock feature. "This is really exciting," he said, pulling out one or two more rocks. "I'm sure this was originally a grotto. Look at these rocks here, they've been carefully shaped."

He went on to tell them that grottos often fell into ruin if they weren't properly maintained. "It looks as though this was a particularly fine one," he added.

Dad didn't look at all enthusiastic.

Toby's father had poked his head into a big hole. "It's very wet in here," he said.

Poppy couldn't contain her excitement any longer. "We think that's because when the grotto collapsed it blocked a natural spring," she cried. "The natural spring that must have once fed the lake."

"What?" Dad was looking interested now.

Poppy and Toby explained the ideas they'd been discussing.

As they talked, Toby's father paced up and down in excitement. As soon as they'd finished he said, "Of course, of course. It all makes sense." He slapped Poppy's dad on the back. "If what they're saying is correct – and it won't take much to prove it – your troubles are over, Jim."

Poppy's dad looked stunned. "It would certainly explain those magnificent alder trees," he said. "Alders grow particularly well in damp conditions."

Then Mum arrived with Katy, whose face and hands had just been cleaned of chocolate. Colour flooded back into Dad's cheeks and his words were tumbling out as he explained all about the spring to his wife.

"This could be the answer to our prayers," cried Mum.

"And this lovely green corner was nothing to do with all the rain we've had – it was because of the blocked spring!" Dad chuckled. "I'm going to start looking into it straight away."

Then everyone was talking and laughing at once.

Poppy picked Archie up so he could be a part of it. "It's all thanks to Little Chick," she said.

Chapter 13

Archie
New Friends

Archie was quite bewildered. Apparently he was some sort of hero. He didn't understand what he'd done – apart from falling down that dark, damp hole. *And how would that have helped anyone?* he wondered.

A man called Mr Dixon, who lived over the fence, had been pleased with him too. He said he'd saved him having expensive pipe-work carried out in his garden. *But I've never been there*, thought Archie.

Whatever it was, Archie was enjoying all

the attention. And there had been a lot going on for him to watch.

His rock feature, which was apparently now called a grotto, had been taken apart by Toby's father. Poppy and Toby had helped too.

They were rebuilding it and making his hidey-hole much bigger. So big that now Poppy would be able to go in it with him as well.

Archie eyed the water trickling out of a hole in the rocks just to one side of it. It splashed into a sort of stone dish and then ran into the lake. "I'll have to remember to keep clear of that," he said, with a shudder. He really didn't like getting wet.

His brother- and sister-ducks liked swimming where the water flowed in. Like Archie, they were getting bigger now. All their white feathers had grown and they looked just like smaller versions of their parents.

Archie looked proudly at his own white feathers. He had a nice pattern of black ones on his neck now and some rather fine black tail feathers appearing. He checked his reflection in the lake every day and had recently discovered that he also had a natty red comb beginning to grow on his head.

More visitors had started coming into the gardens. Archie liked the visitors now – they often said he was cute. And they were all interested in the discovery of his grotto.

Poppy was happier now, even though she had to go back to this place called school on Monday. She said she'd come to see him before she went – and then as soon as she got back every day.

Archie was intrigued by what Mr Dixon and Mum were building. They'd been at it for a couple of days now. "It looks like a big duck-house," said Archie to himself. "I guess they must be getting some new –

large – ducks. But why are they putting all that wire up?"

Poppy had been helping as well today. She seemed excited. "OK, Little Chick, it's all ready now," she said to him. "What do you think?"

Archie looked up at her with his head on one side.

"It's a chicken house – and it's for you," she said.

For me? thought Archie. *But why?*

Then Dad called over to them. "They've arrived."

"Great!" cried Poppy, and she, Mum and Mr Dixon ran off towards the house.

Archie walked slowly through the open wire door towards his new home. "It's huge," he said, peering in the doorway. "Am I going to grow that big?"

He'd just ventured inside to examine it when he heard Poppy calling him. "Little Chick. Come and see what we've got."

He hurried out to see Poppy and her mother carrying big boxes. Mr Dixon was pushing Dad in his wheelchair and he had a box on his lap. They put the boxes down inside the run and closed the wire gate.

More ducks? wondered Archie. *But why are they in here? I thought this was my home.*

Poppy picked Archie up. "You won't have to stay in the run. It's just until the others get used to it here."

Archie was even more puzzled.

Then Mum opened the first box. Out popped three beautiful white heads with black neck markings. And they all had striking red combs.

Archie's heart leapt as they jumped, clucking, straight out into the run. Chickens! He knew immediately what they were. He didn't need to be told.

There were three slightly bigger ones in the second box and the six chickens began strutting round the run, scratching and pecking at the earth.

They're beautiful! he thought.

Then Mr Dixon opened the third box and this chicken was somehow different. He was the same colouring but he was taller, prouder. And he had the most wonderful black tail. This chicken was magnificent!

"There you are, Little Chick," said Poppy. "Some friends to share your new home with you. They're the same breed as you – Light Sussex. We didn't know what breed you were until your feathers started to grow."

Archie turned to look at her with his beak open and his eyes wide. He felt suddenly shy of these magnificent, beautiful birds.

"Light Sussex are one of the oldest breeds in Britain," Jim told him. "You're one of a very historic breed."

So as well as being a hero, I'm historic too, thought Archie. It was a lot to take in. He just sat in Poppy's arms watching the chickens exploring the run.

Poppy seemed to sense that he felt shy. She bent down with him. "See, there are six hens – they're female chickens. The three smaller ones are only a bit older than you. And you see that handsome one over there?" She pointed to the large, proud bird. "He's a cockerel. You'll look just like him when you're grown up."

Archie couldn't believe it. *Will I really be that handsome?*

Poppy put him down in the run and he suddenly lost his shyness. He ran over to them.

The chickens all looked up and came

crowding round him. They were so friendly, so pleased to see him.

"Hey, you guys," said Archie. "What say we scratch some earth together? See what we can find?"

This time everyone wanted to join him.

Archie was so happy. He'd always be fond of his duck foster-family, even if they were always out on the lake. And Poppy would always be his very special friend. But now he felt like he belonged. He had real friends that wanted to hang around with him, liked doing the same things. Chickens, just like him!

He'd never be lonely again.

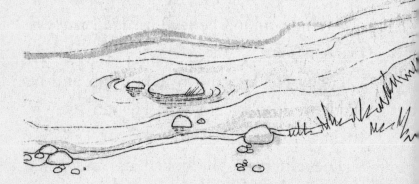